Disney's A CHRISTMAS CAROL

BAH, HUMBUG!

By Ebenezer Scrooge
Based on the classic story by Charles Dickens
Based on the screenplay by Robert Zemeckis
Produced by Steve Starkey, Robert Zemeckis, Jack Rapke
Directed by Robert Zemeckis

Printed in the United States of America
First Edition 1 3 5 7 9 10 6 8 4 2
Library of Congress Catalog Card Number on file.
ISBN 978-1-4231-2211-1

Visit disneybooks.com
Disney.com/ChristmasCarol

Disney PRESS
New York

$\mathcal{B}$ah! Fiend! This book is a **private** work. Belonging to **me**, Ebenezer Scrooge. It is meant for **my** eyes only. Close this book and begone! Go! Off with you!

So, you are not one to listen to reason, then. Very well. After all, as a child there were times when even *I* chose not to heed the warnings of others. But those times were few and far between. Mostly, I was an obedient youngster. And I discovered very early on what would make me happy. Not fame, nor family, nor silly holidays. Fortune was all I needed.

By the time I was a young man, I was well on my way to riches. I worked hard and saved every penny I could. I made time for nothing but my job. Not even my love of the beautiful Belle got in the way of work. And when other fools at my workplace celebrated childish holidays, well, I refused to join them.

Disgusted by the laziness of others, I went into business with the only person in London who shared my views on hard work. My new partner's name was Marley.

Marley passed away some time ago. Some say it was the work itself that did him in. I say, bah! Hard work never killed a man. What did him in were the few days of rest he took toward the end. He would have felt much better had he only pushed himself harder.

    With Marley gone, I have mostly been alone. And I like it that way. What need has any man for others? I have the grand home I have worked hard for. And there is not a voice to disturb me when I arrive there after a day's work. Lonesome, you say? Bah! I find it peaceful and comforting!

Still, some fools would like me to spend less time alone. My nephew Fred invites me to dinner every year. Just once a year. For the wretched Christmas holiday. Bah! I say. Humbug!

Besides, I am not as alone as Fred suspects. I spend each day with my clerk, Bob Cratchit, in my countinghouse. I try to show him the right way to live his life. But he does not listen. If only he worked harder—and saved more! He could be just like me! Instead, he chooses to live in a hovel with his family!

They call Cratchit's son Tiny Tim. I suppose it is because he is small and sickly. If there is one reason for Cratchit to wise up and change, it is this child.

But even his weak son does not inspire Cratchit. He dares to ask for extra days off during Christmastide. Bah!

The dreaded holiday is fast approaching. The snow has begun to fall on London streets. Carolers are already singing. Windows are decked with holly. Bah! Humbug!

This is, without question, the most foolish time of the year.

꩜ Most fools have no idea that mistletoe is poisonous—as is the season itself.

꩜ Do you have any idea how much coal and wood is wasted on yuletide fires? Bah!

The selfsame fools who claim they do not have money for clothes hang their stockings by the fire to be filled with treats they cannot afford. They should try wearing the stockings instead!

So many complain about the cost of food, yet once a year they waste their money on an expensive Christmas goose!

Many have tried to change me. I have been called cruel. I am feared, and I know it. I care not for my fellow man. After all, what has he ever done for me? And I most certainly do not care for Christmas.

Now and forever I say, bah!

Bah, humbug!